Mr. Buzz
the Beeman

By Allan Ahlberg
Illustrated by Faith Jaques

GOLDEN PRESS • NEW YORK
Western Publishing Company, Inc.
Racine, Wisconsin

First published in the United Kingdom by Puffin Books/Kestrel Books.
Published in the U.S.A. in 1982.

Library of Congress Catalog Card Number: 81-84172
ISBN 0-307-31703-X / ISBN 0-307-61703-3 (lib. bdg.)
A B C D E F G H I J

There was once a beeman
named Mr. Buzz.
Mr. Buzz lived in a cottage
with his wife and children.
They had a cow, a cat, two canaries,
three goldfish, five beehives—

and a hundred and fifty thousand bees!

Every day the bees worked hard.
They flew from flower to flower.
They took nectar back to the hives
and made the honey.
They were as busy as bees.

Every day Mr. Buzz and his family
worked hard, too.
Mr. Buzz took the honey from the hives.
Mrs. Buzz put it into the honey jars.
Master Buzz made labels
for the honey jars.
Miss Buzz stuck them on.

One morning Mr. Buzz
was making a new beehive.
Suddenly he saw a terrible thing.
Some of the bees were in a swarm—
and they were flying away!

When bees fly off in a swarm,
they almost never come back.
Mr. Buzz knew this.
"The bees are buzzing off!" he cried.
So Mr. Buzz and his family
put on their bee hats
and their bee gloves,
picked up a bee basket—
and went chasing after the bees.

The bees flew down the road.

A mailman was riding by on his bike.

"The bees are buzzing off!" cried Mr. Buzz.

"The little rascals," the mailman said.

"I will help you catch them!"

The bees flew over a farmer's field,
with Mr. Buzz and his family
and the mailman on his bike
all chasing after them.

The farmer and his dog
were in the field.
"The bees are buzzing off!"
cried Mr. Buzz.

"The little scamps," the farmer said.
"I will help you catch them!"
The bees flew by the river,
with Mr. Buzz and his family,
and the mailman on his bike,

and the farmer with his dog
all chasing after them.

The little devils!

A fisherman with his rod and line
was sitting on the bank.
   "The bees are buzzing off!"
cried Mr. Buzz.
   "The little devils," the fisherman said.
"I will help you catch them!"

The bees flew past the village school,
with Mr. Buzz and his family,
and the mailman on his bike,
and the farmer with his dog,
and the fisherman with his rod and line
all chasing after them.

The teacher and the children
were in the playground.

"The bees are buzzing off!"
cried Mr. Buzz.

"The little beasts," the teacher said.
"We will help you catch them!"

The bees flew by the village church,
with Mr. Buzz and his family,
and the mailman on his bike,
and the farmer with his dog,
and the fisherman with his rod and line,
and the teacher and the children
all chasing after them.

A wedding party was standing
on the steps.

"The bees are buzzing off!"
cried Mr. Buzz.

"The little scalawags," the bride said.
"We will help you catch them!"

The bees flew *up* the road,
with Mr. Buzz and his family,
and the mailman on his bike,
and the farmer with his dog,
and the fisherman with his rod and line,
and the teacher and the children,

and the bride and groom
and wedding guests and bridesmaids
all chasing after them.

Suddenly Mr. Buzz saw
where the bees were going.
"Those bees are not buzzing off!"
he cried. "They are buzzing back again!"

And so they were—
straight back into the new hive
that Mr. Buzz had made.

Then everyone said,
"The little rascals!"
"The little scamps!"
"The little devils!"
"The little beasts!"
"The little scalawags!"

After that Mr. Buzz and his family,
and the mailman on his bike,
and the farmer with his dog,
and the fisherman with his rod and line,
and the teacher and the children,
and the bride and groom

and wedding guests and bridesmaids—
all sat down in the garden
for honey and tea.

"Our bees made this," said Mr. Buzz
as he passed the honey jars around.

And everyone said . . .

The End